It's five years since Ben Tennyson last transformed into aliens and fought crime with his cousin Gwen and their Grandpa Max.

Now 15 years old, Ben is once again forced to turn to the Omnitrix to help fight a new and more sinister threat – the HighBreed, DNAliens and the Forever Knights, who team up to take over the world.

The watch-like Omnitrix has re-programmed itself and has a complete set of ten, brand new alien choices for Ben to get to grips with. Helped by his cousin Gwen with her magical powers and Ben's former enemy, Kevin E. Levin, Ben is soon all set to go hero once again!

## NOW READ ON . . .

# EGMONT

*We bring stories to life*

This edition first published in Great Britain 2010
by Egmont UK Limited
239 Kensington High Street
London W8 6SA

Adapted by Barry Hutchison

1 3 5 7 9 10 8 6 4 2

Printed and bound in Great Britain

The Forest Stewardship Council (FSC) is an international,
non-governmental organisation dedicated to promoting
responsible management of the world's forests. FSC operates
a system of forest certification and product labelling that
allows consumers to identify wood and wood-based products
from well-managed forests.

For more information about Egmont's paper buying policy,
please visit www.egmont.co.uk/ethicalpublishing
For more information about the FSC, please visit their
website at www.fsc.org

# BEN 10 ALIEN FORCE

## PLUMBERS' HELPERS

# CHAPTER ONE

## HELEN AND MANNY

**F**ootsteps echoed through the empty halls of a locked-up sewerage plant, faster and faster, as if someone was running for their life. A man burst from the shadows, his eyes bulging as he glanced back over his shoulder.

Whirling around, the man raised a blaster gun. The hall lit up as he fired shots into the darkness. He allowed himself to catch his breath. Nothing there. He was safe – for now.

The disguise was slowing him down. He reached up and tore off his face. It came away easily, revealing the man to be an undercover DNAlien – a henchman of the evil HighBreed.

A laser blast scorched the air by his deformed head. The alien was off and running at once, ducking and weaving through the shadows, frantically trying to avoid his pursuer. As he ran, he twisted and took aim with his gun. But before he could pull the trigger, he slipped on a patch of spilled oil.

The alien slid across the floor. He struggled to stay upright, but it was a losing battle. He quickly lost his balance and came crashing to the ground. The gun slipped from his fingers and clattered noisily across the floor.

The alien scuttled forwards, its claw-like

hands scrabbling for the weapon. Just as he reached it, another energy blast tore through the air. The gun exploded in a shower of bright blue sparks.

The DNAlien leaped back to his feet. His single bulging eye scanned the shadows. Nothing moved. Whoever was chasing him had ducked back out of sight. Wasting no time, the alien turned on his heels and darted off in search of a way out.

The inside of the plant was a maze of narrow, winding passageways. Losing his pursuer shouldn't be too difficult. All he had to do was keep his wits about him and not run into a . . . trap?

The alien stumbled to a stop. Up ahead, two red lights blinked into life. He watched them grow steadily brighter, then realised – too late – what they were. A large van was reversing directly towards him!

Before the DNAlien could run again, two bands of purple energy wrapped around his arms, handcuffing him. He writhed and wrestled against the bonds, as they slowly pulled him towards the back of the van.

When the alien was almost at the vehicle, the rear door slid upwards. The creature squealed and struggled when he spotted what was waiting for him inside the van: a Null Void Projector.

With a final, deafening scream, the alien creature was dragged into the van and sucked into the dark, empty, endless wasteland of the Null Void.

The scream was still hanging in the air when two figures emerged from inside the vehicle. The larger of the two curled all four of his arms, flexing his powerful muscles. The four-armed alien looked down at his partner, and grinned. 'Another one bites the dust!'

The van rattled along a city street, its headlights shining like beacons in the evening gloom. The larger alien was behind the wheel. He was from a race known as the Tetramands. Many years ago, Ben had been able to use the Omnitrix to transform into an alien just like him – the super-strong Four Arms.

'Hey, Helen. Did you see the look on that DNAlien's face when we roped him?' the big alien laughed. 'That was one freaked out . . .' He noticed his partner wasn't laughing along with him. 'What?'

In the passenger seat, Helen was gazing out of the window. She was also an alien – a member of the lightning-fast Kinceleran race. Kinceleran DNA was also stored in the Omnitrix, allowing Ben to transform into the alien he called XLR8 a few years back.

'Forget it, Manny,' said Helen, briefly glancing in her partner's direction.

Manny began to prod her with one of his free arms. 'Helen, come on. Talk to me.'

'Quit it!' Helen snapped.

'Come on.'

'Stop. I said no,' Helen said, slapping his

hand away.

'Ow!' Manny yelped. 'What is with you?'

'Nothing's with me. I just . . .' Helen turned back to the window and gazed into the dark. 'I wish Pierce were here.'

'Yeah, I know,' Manny nodded. 'Me too.'

'Yeah, right.'

'What do you mean?' asked Manny. 'Your brother and I – '

'Argued over every single mission,' said Helen, cutting him off. She pulled a face and began to imitate Manny and Pierce's voices. 'Who's in charge? Do it this way. No, my plan's much better.'

Manny hesitated. 'OK, yeah. We disagreed. But now that he's . . .' He cut the sentence short when he saw the sadness in Helen's eyes. 'Helen, I'm just trying to do what we all agreed to do,' he said, softly. 'Fry every DNAlien we can find.'

A piercing alarm rang out from the van's

dashboard and a display screen lit up. A trio of red dots flashed in the middle of the monitor.

'Three of them, and they're close,' said Helen, quickly.

'Where?'

Helen studied the display. 'Back at the sewerage plant.'

### SCREEEEEECH!

Manny wrenched the wheel and pulled up the handbrake, sending the van into a sharp turn. He gritted his teeth and slammed his foot down on the accelerator pedal. The tyres squealed on the tarmac, as the vehicle roared back towards the sewerage plant.

Back at the plant, Helen and Manny were searching the grounds. A high-tech, alien-looking gadget in Manny's hand flashed wildly.

'Can't get a lock on them,' he muttered. 'Stupid machine.'

'Want me to try?' Helen offered.

'No,' Manny hissed. 'Sssh!'

Slowly, he waved the machine around, left to right, scanning for the aliens. At last, the outline of three figures appeared on the built-in display screen. Manny adjusted the controls and voices began to crackle over the gadget's speaker system.

'Are you sure you know what you're doing, Sherlock?' asked the first voice. It was male, probably around seventeen years old.

'For once can you keep your mouth shut and open your eyes? Just follow the blueprints,' sighed a second voice. This one was also male, but it sounded a couple of years younger than the first.

'Would you both be quiet?' said a female voice. 'It could be a guard or something.'

'I'd swear the alien ran into here,' said the first voice.

'Well,' replied the girl, 'there's no sign of him now.'

On his screen, Manny saw the older boy bend down and pick something up off the ground. 'Oo-hoo-hoo,' said the boy, 'come and check this out.'

A hiss of static burst from the speaker on Manny's scanner, making it impossible to hear what the boy said next.

'What did he say?' frowned Helen.

'Doesn't matter,' Manny replied, slipping the scanner back on to his belt. He clenched all four of his powerful fists and cracked his knuckles, noisily. 'Let's dust 'em!'

# CHAPTER TWO

## TRACKING THEIR PREY

**H**elen caught Manny by one of his arms. 'We can't. The Eradicannon needs more time to re-charge.' She glanced over to the van. 'How about we follow them instead? Maybe they'll lead us to a whole nest of DNAliens.'

She turned back to her partner, but he was already on the move, scaling a building to get a better shot at his prey.

'Manny,' she sighed, setting off after him.

With a grunt, Manny pulled himself up on to the roof. He darted to the edge and peered down. The three aliens were there. They were in human disguises, and standing beside a green car.

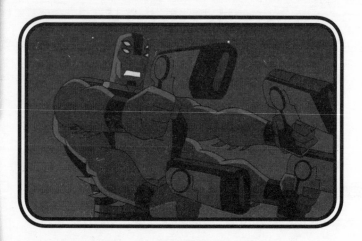

Reaching into the holsters on his belt, Manny drew four laser pistols and took aim. He held his breath, lining each shot up perfectly.

A blur of speed shot across the roof. Helen stopped directly in front of him, preventing him from taking the shot. In a flash, she stripped him of the weapons.

'You just never listen to me, do you?' Helen scowled.

Down on the ground, the three figures were climbing into the car. Manny watched with dismay as the engine began to roar.

'They're getting away!' he complained.

'No,' said Helen, extending her wrist. 'They aren't.'

**SHNINK!**

A round green locator tool shot from a gadget on Helen's arm. It spun through the air like a flying disk. Just before the car pulled away, the locator disk attached itself to the rear bumper. Now, no matter where the three aliens might go, Helen and Manny would be able to track and follow them.

Later, back at their headquarters, Helen was sitting alone. She was watching the monitor of a hand-held video player. On screen, her brother, Pierce, was speaking directly into the camera.

'August tenth,' he said. 'We zapped another DNAlien. Third one this month. Only . . .' Pierce hesitated and glanced down at the ground. 'Something weird happened. We had the creep cornered. I got my energy lash wrapped around him, but just before Manny hooked 'em, he flashed a Plumber's badge.

'Figured it had to be fake, but now I don't know. What if it was real? What if we were wrong about – '

A door opening on the roof behind him cut him off. On screen, Pierce turned to see Helen emerge from the door, with Manny right behind her.

'Helen, what is with you?' Manny asked her. 'Every night you're up here.'

'Sometimes I like to look at the stars,' Helen explained. 'You know, think about what's out there.'

'Out there?' Manny spluttered. 'Out there is why we're all contaminated freaks. It's why we're kicking alien butt so nobody has to go through what happened to us.'

Pierce gave a sigh and walked over to join the others. 'Would you two stop it?' he shouted. 'Every day it's the same fight. I can't babysit you forever, you know?'

The picture on screen froze as the recording came to an end. Helen touched the on-screen picture of her brother. 'I know,' she whispered.

The door to the room slid open and Helen looked up. Manny stood in the doorway, beckoning to her. 'Come here,' he said. 'I wanna show you something.'

She hopped down from her chair and followed him through to another room. Monitors and complicated alien machinery covered all the walls.

'I fed the thermo scans from the sewerage plant into one of Pierce's computers,' Manny explained. He pushed a few buttons and looked up at the largest of the display screens.

Absolutely nothing appeared to happen.

'Wow,' said Helen, sarcastically. 'Great. I am so impressed.'

'Stupid machine,' growled Manny, thumping a fist down on to the control console. The screen flickered for a moment, and then the silhouettes of the three figures they'd seen at the plant appeared.

Static flashed across the monitor for a few seconds, and then the outlines were replaced by images of three humans. Helen and Manny didn't know it, but the humans were Ben Tennyson, his cousin Gwen, and their friend, Kevin E. Levin.

'Those are aliens?' frowned Helen. 'They look human.'

'They must be wearing disguises. I would've caught them if you hadn't gone and stopped me.'

'They outnumbered us,' Helen reminded him. 'I stopped you from starting a fight that we would never have been able to win.'

'Well, Pierce would definitely have done it,' Manny snapped.

Helen spun around to face him. Anger burned in the green centres of her eyes. 'No, he wouldn't. And don't you dare use him as an excuse! Pierce found all this alien junk and made it work. Pierce brought us together. And when Pierce was in charge, we were careful. The one time we weren't . . .' Her voice broke off as tears began to roll down her cheeks.

Manny sighed. 'I'm sorry, OK? Look, tomorrow we'll track their signal. We'll take it slow. We'll be careful. Just the way Pierce was.'

Helen nodded her head once, then walked out of the lab, wiping the tears from her eyes. Manny watched her go, then turned back to the monitor.

'But once we find them,' he said to himself, 'then we'll handle things my way.'

The next night, Kevin's car weaved through the late-evening traffic. None of the three occupants of the vehicle had even noticed the van following a hundred metres or so behind them.

Inside the van, Helen fiddled with the controls of the hand-held scanner.

'What are they doing?' asked Manny from

the driver's seat.

'I can't lock in on them, but it sounds like they're arguing.' Helen glanced across at her partner. 'Do you think they know that we're tailing them?'

A grin spread across Manny's face. 'Why don't we make sure?'

Up ahead, the car was pulling into a petrol station. Manny wound down his window and thrust an arm out. Helen realised he was holding a blaster gun.

'Manny, no!' she cried, but her partner didn't listen. Manny squeezed the trigger, sending bright bolts of blue energy screaming along the street.

Before the blasts could hit the car, a large petrol tanker pulled out behind it. The laser bolts hit the wheels of the truck, sending it into a spin. The back end of the tanker swung wide, tearing through the petrol station and smashing one of the pumps.

The front end of the truck crashed hard into an oncoming car. Flames began to flicker across the engine bay and into the driver's cab.

Leaping from Kevin's car, Ben spotted the shattered fuel pump. Petrol was quickly flooding out, forming an expanding puddle over the forecourt.

'If that tanker goes up, we're talking about a major bonfire,' he said.

Kevin jumped from the car and began sprinting towards the front of the truck. 'I'll get the driver,' he cried.

'And I've got the truck,' nodded Ben. 'Gwen, give us cover.'

'I'm on it,' Gwen told him, clambering from the back seat of the car. The two of them ran towards the back of the tanker, neither one noticing the van screeching to a halt a few metres behind them.

'I can't believe you did that!' Helen yelled at Manny.

'So what?' scowled Manny. 'They're getting away.'

By the time Manny unclipped his seatbelt, Helen had already left the van.

A crowd of spectators had gathered near the truck. They watched on, frightened, but desperate to see what was going to happen next. Gwen had some bad news for them. She blasted the ground in front of the onlookers with her energy powers. The tarmac road cracked and curved upwards, forming a solid wall in front of the flaming truck.

Meanwhile, Kevin had almost reached the driver's cab. As he ran, he brushed his fingers against the side of the steel tanker, absorbing its strength. By the time he reached the door of the cab, his body was covered entirely in living metal.

'How come I always get the easy jobs?' he wondered, as he tore the door off its hinges.

He pulled the unconscious driver from his seat and hoisted him over his shoulder. Petrol flooded around his feet and Kevin started to run. Sparks rained down from the burning cab. Kevin pushed himself to move even faster, but it was too late.

**WHOOSH!**

Kevin heard the petrol catch light. Even in his powerful metal form he could feel the burning heat of the huge fireball as it raced up behind him, the flames getting ever closer.

# CHAPTER THREE

# TEAM-MATE TROUBLES

The flames licked at Kevin's back. He knew the fire couldn't hurt him in his current form, but the driver would be burned to a crisp. There was only one chance. He had to try something he'd never attempted before.

Throwing himself into a forward roll, Kevin reached out with one hand and touched the hard concrete ground. With his other hand he took hold of the unconscious truck driver's bare arm.

Kevin's shiny metallic surface gave way to rough, grey stone. He almost cheered with relief when he saw that the driver, too, was becoming covered in a tough concrete exterior. The flames engulfed them as the fire tore across the forecourt towards the broken petrol pump, but the stone saved them both from being hurt.

Once the inferno had rushed harmlessly past them, Kevin stood up and nodded to Ben. 'Your turn,' he said.

Ben didn't waste any time in activating the Omnitrix. The familiar swirl of green energy wrapped around him, transforming him into the moth-like Big Chill.

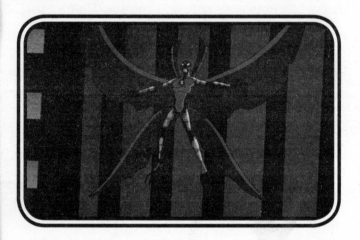

A short distance away, Helen watched in amazement as Big Chill flew over the burning petrol station, breathing freezing fog down over the flames. As the frozen air hit the forecourt, the fire was snuffed out. In just a few seconds, the whole petrol station was encased in ice.

Kevin set the truck driver down on the ground. Using his powers, he returned him back to normal. All traces of the stone that had saved the driver from the fire quickly disappeared.

'Hey, you!' bellowed a voice.

Kevin looked up to see Manny standing in the middle of the street. He had Kevin's car held above his head, and a wicked glint in all four of his eyes.

'Catch!' Manny cried. He hurled the car with all his strength.

Kevin's eyes went wide as he saw his car hurtling through the air towards him. 'Not my ride!' he groaned.

**SLAM!**

The front of the car hit Kevin in the chest. It knocked him off his feet and smashed him into the side of the now frozen truck.

'Kevin!' cried Gwen, who had seen the whole thing. She hurried over to help him, but before she could get there, something began to circle around her at tremendous speed. Faster and faster it went, until Gwen was standing in the centre of a whirling tornado.

The wind whipped her into the air, sending her flipping end over end, around and around, until she didn't know which way was up. Then, just as suddenly as it had started, the tornado stopped. Gwen screamed as she realised she was plunging head-first towards the ground.

Big Chill spun around at the sound of his cousin's cry. Taking a deep breath, he blasted out a stream of frosty air. An ice-slide formed below Gwen just in time, and she slid down to a safe, but chilly, landing.

Over by the petrol tanker, Kevin wasn't so lucky. A hulking fist slammed him hard against the ground, shattering the concrete. As Kevin slumped unconscious, his rock-hard protective coating vanished, leaving him completely at Manny's mercy.

The four-armed alien lifted Kevin by the back of the neck and studied him as if he were an insect. He barely noticed Helen rushing over to join him.

'You see that?' she asked. 'They saved that guy.'

'Who cares?' Manny shrugged. 'One of them's hurt. Now's our chance to take them.'

'No way,' said Helen, glancing over to where Big Chill was transforming back into Ben.

'Not until we talk.'

In a heartbeat she zoomed away, leaving Manny to drag Kevin over to the van.

Gwen was shivering as Ben helped her back to her feet. Neither of them noticed the van driving past them, or could have guessed what was inside.

'W-where's K-Kevin,' said Gwen through chattering teeth.

Ben sighed heavily and stared off into the night. 'Gone,' he said.

Back at his house, Ben was on the warpath. He paced the floor of his bedroom, ranting furiously.

'And what really bugs me is one of them was an XLR8,' he complained. 'I mean, I used to turn into that species. None of it makes any sense.' He looked across to Gwen, who was sitting quietly on the bed. 'Gwen? Jump in at any time.'

'Ssh,' Gwen hissed. 'I'm concentrating.'

Ben frowned. 'On what?'

'I'm at one with the cosmic mana, feeling the energy of the Universe flowing around and through me,' Gwen replied, casually. She had her eyes closed. When she opened them, they glowed with mystical energy.

'Groovy,' Ben replied. 'Why?'

'So that I can locate Kevin. Which I have.'
The pink glow faded and her eyes returned to
normal. She jumped up off the bed. 'Now all we
have to do is rescue him.'

'Oh,' Ben scowled. 'Is that all?'

A bright yellow ball of energy floated
above the floor of Manny and Helen's
headquarters. Inside lay Kevin – trapped and
helpless, but wide awake. Like Ben, Manny was
pacing the floor.

'What were you thinking?' he yelled at
Helen. 'We had them on the ropes. We could've
nailed three monsters at once!'

'Monsters?' snorted Kevin. 'That's a laugh
coming from a Halloween reject like you!'

Manny flexed his muscles and narrowed
his eyes. 'Sounds like the alien dirt bag is

asking for another fight.'

'Let me out of this bubble,' growled Kevin. 'Then we'll see what you've got.'

'Quiet,' snapped Helen. The tone of her voice took them both by surprise. 'You sound like a couple of young children fighting in the school playground.'

'I'm not anything like him,' said Kevin and Manny at the same time.

Furious, Manny stormed over to the bubble and pushed a hand through it. His powerful fingers wrapped around Kevin's face and began to pull. Kevin hissed with pain.

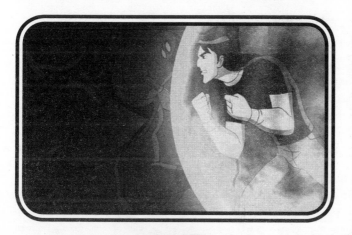

'Manny, stop that. It's not a mask,' Helen cried out. 'You're hurting him!'

'That's my face,' snarled Kevin, pulling free of Manny's grip.

'It doesn't matter,' Manny bellowed. 'He's an alien, and I say we feed him to the Eradicannon.'

Kevin patted his face, making sure it was still intact. 'The . . . uh . . . Eradi-what?'

Manny gestured towards a nearby alien gadget. 'A disintegrator beam. It turns scum like you into dust.'

'That's not a disintegrator, you dufus!' Kevin laughed. 'It's a Null Void Projector.'

Manny frowned. 'A Null Void . . . what?'

'Probably a Mark One,' continued Kevin, looking more closely at the device. 'It's a museum piece. And you are a pinhead.'

Drawing his guns, Manny blasted the energy bubble. Inside, Kevin cried out in pain as he was thrown violently around. His head slammed hard against the wall of the prison, and he slumped down into an unconscious heap in the bubble.

'Why did you do that?' gasped Helen.

'He was getting on my nerves.'

'What if you're wrong, Manny?' Helen asked. 'What if he's not an alien?'

'You saw his powers, he's gotta be an alien,' replied Manny. He picked up a hand-held device from a tabletop. 'I'll prove it to you.'

The gadget bleeped as Manny switched it on. A list of alien races appeared on the device's screen. He scrolled through them, trying to find a match.

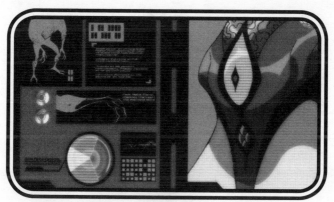

'Gotta be one like him in here,' he said, flicking through dozens of different aliens.

'Manny, listen to me,' Helen pleaded. 'That guy in there, whatever he is, has a Plumber's badge.'

'So?'

'There was something in Pierce's diary. One of the aliens we nailed last summer – he had one, too.'

'Big deal,' Manny shrugged. 'If he has a badge, it's a fake. Him and his pals, they're all alien villains.'

'Then why would they save that driver? Why did they stop the truck from exploding?'

'I don't know and I don't care. They're all aliens,' he nodded towards the Null Void Projector. 'And you know exactly what we do with aliens.'

# CHAPTER FOUR

## FIVE WAY FIGHT

A few miles across town from Helen and Manny's base, an overcrowded bus slowly chugged its way along a busy street. On the back seats, Ben and Gwen waited impatiently for the driver to speed up.

'What kind of heroes take the bus?' Gwen muttered.

'Neither of us is old enough to drive. What do you want me to do?' asked Ben. He held his hand to his ear, as if he were talking on the telephone. 'Hi, Mum. We have to go fight some aliens. Can you give us a ride?'

Gwen shook her head. 'OK, whatever. I'm just worried, that's all.'

'About Kevin?'

'Well, yeah, what else? We need to find

him before . . . You know. Before something bad happens.' She smiled, bashfully. 'Not that I care or anything. I mean, come on – how could anyone care about a person who's that rude and unreliable, and . . . and annoying? It's ridiculous.' She gave her cousin a slap on the arm. 'How could you even think of saying something like that?'

'Actually,' Ben coughed, 'I didn't say anything at all.'

Gwen felt her cheeks go red. She turned and looked out at the buildings creeping by outside. Why couldn't this thing go any faster?

Helen studied the screen of the alien tracker. The shape of the bus was outlined on the display in red.

'Aliens,' she announced. 'And they are

headed this way. We need to get ready.'

Manny picked up a blaster pistol and the energy snare weapon he had used to capture the DNAlien at the sewerage plant. Helen zipped speedily around the lab, picking up her own weapons.

'OK,' nodded Manny, when they were both ready. 'Let's go!'

A minute or so later, the alien-hunters stepped through the front door of their headquarters and out into the cool evening air.

'How close are they?' Manny asked.

'Very,' replied a voice, before Helen had even opened her mouth.

Manny and Helen turned to see Ben and Gwen standing nearby. Pink energy crackled between Gwen's fingertips. 'Now,' she said, 'give us back our friend.'

Ben raised an eyebrow. 'Friend?'

Gwen blushed again. 'Team-mate, co-worker, whatever. Could we not talk about this at some other time?'

'Hey,' Ben protested, 'I'm not the one who always – '

Helen fired an energy blast at the wall above the heroes. Rubble rained down on Ben, knocking him to the ground. He lay there, eyes closed, groaning in pain.

Gwen bent down to help him, but not before she unleashed an attack of her own. Her power beam hit Manny directly in the chest, sending him stumbling backwards. The battle had begun!

Inside his bubble prison, Kevin was waking up. He groaned as he heard the screeches of the laser weapons outside.

'Sounds like my rescuers need rescuing,' he said. From his pocket, he pulled out a few coins. Concentrating, he absorbed their properties. They barely contained enough metal for him to cover his hand in a dull copper coating. 'Huh,' he muttered. 'I guess this will have to do.'

Summoning all his strength, Kevin drove a punch down, hard, against the floor of the bubble. Pain shot through him, burning like fire across his body. Still he pushed, until he felt his fingers emerge through the bottom of the weird energy prison.

Just . . . a little . . . more, he thought, forcing his arm further through the wall of the bubble. With a triumphant yell, he found what he was looking for. His metallic fingers wrapped around the prison projector, and squeezed. As the device shattered, the bubble disappeared with a **POP**.

'Huh,' he smiled, getting his breath back. 'The four-armed freak is not the only tough guy around.'

He crossed to the wall and touched one of the solid iron pipes that ran from floor to ceiling. The pain in his arm faded as his whole body took on the dull sheen of the metal. Kevin smiled, grimly. It was time for him to get his own back.

Outside, Gwen had dragged the still-unconscious Ben behind a low wall. Energy blasts rained down around them, pinning them in place.

'Come on, Ben,' she pleaded. 'I need a little help here.'

Manny and Helen stopped firing as the wall behind them exploded outwards. A metal figure emerged, his face a mask of anger.

'Nothing like a little iron in your diet to perk you right up,' Kevin growled, setting his sights on Manny.

The four-armed alien launched himself at Kevin, his enormous fists raised.

'Manny, wait!' Helen cried, but her partner was no longer listening to her. His first punch caught Kevin on the side of the head, sending him spinning on to the pavement.

Kevin recovered quickly. He caught Manny's next punch and twisted the alien's arm. A metal elbow slammed into Manny's cheek, making him cry out in shock. He didn't notice Kevin's uppercut until it hit against the bottom of his jaw.

Staggering backwards, Manny shook the cobwebs from his head. He tensed his bulging muscles. If it was a fight this guy wanted, it was a fight he would get!

Meanwhile, Helen was doing her best to keep Gwen and Ben trapped behind the wall. She squeezed the trigger of her blaster gun.

**BLAM, BLAM, BLAM!**

A power beam streaked towards her, but

Helen was too fast. She dodged sideways and continued her attack.

'Stand still, will you?' growled Gwen, unleashing more energy bolts.

Down on the ground, Ben opened his eyes. His head ached badly. He groaned, rubbing a bump on the back of his skull. 'I've got to start wearing a helmet.'

Groggily, Ben pulled himself up and squinted down at the Omnitrix. Like everything else at the moment, it looked blurry and indistinct. Ben flicked through the aliens, not noticing that he was staggering out into the middle of the battlefield.

'Ben!' cried Gwen. She moved to catch her cousin, but a sudden volley of laser blasts held her back.

'OK, which one?' drawled Ben, still going through his selection of alien forms. 'Eenie, meenie – '

'Get out of the way!' cried Kevin to Ben, slamming Manny against a wall. Huge chunks of rock broke away from the building and crashed to the ground just centimetres from Ben's feet.

Manny managed to unclip a remote control from his belt and stabbed his fingers against the buttons. His van suddenly came roaring backwards around the corner. As it drew closer, the rear door slid open, revealing that the Null Void Projector had been activated.

Distracted, Gwen turned at the sound of the van's engine. Seizing her chance, Helen whizzed round the girl a few hundred times in the space of a second. Gwen spun round and round on the spot, then fell forwards on to the cold, hard pavement.

Kevin raced over to Gwen as fast as he could, shouting her name. She seemed to be all right, and he knelt beside her, cradling her head. But he was unaware that Manny and Helen were closing in.

'Now,' growled the four-armed alien, activating his energy snare. 'Let's finish 'em!

A band of purple alien energy snaked out from the snare and wrapped around Ben's wrist. A second snare caught his other arm. Ben kicked and struggled, but it was no use. Without the use of his hands he couldn't reach the Omnitrix, and in human form he was nowhere near strong enough to break free of the energy bonds that trapped him.

With a yank, he was lifted off the ground. He felt the Projector pulling him, dragging him in. He was totally helpless. He saw Kevin move to catch him, but by then it was too late. With a lingering scream of terror, Ben was sucked into the van and dragged into the swirling vortex of the Null Void.

# CHAPTER FIVE

# INTO THE NULL VOID

**G**wen and Kevin stared into the swirling heart of the Null Void Projector, too shocked to move. Had it really happened? Was Ben really gone?

'Well, it may be a museum piece, but it did the job on your friend,' crowed Manny. He and Helen had their guns trained on the two heroes. 'And you two are next.'

A faint sound from the Null Void Projector suddenly caught everyone's attention. They all turned in time to see a green hand stretch out from inside the swirling portal. The hand gripped the edge of the machine and began to pull.

The red and yellow head of Swampfire emerged from inside the machine. Amazingly,

Ben had managed to activate the Omnitrix in there! With a heave, the alien hero dragged himself free of the Null Void.

Kevin nodded, impressed. 'I taught him that,' he boasted.

'No you didn't,' Gwen replied.

Swampfire drew himself up to his full height and began to advance on the aliens Manny and Helen.

'It's not a disintegrator,' Helen gasped.

Manny didn't care. He took aim with his blasters. 'Lousy stinking – ' The screech of his laser blasts drowned out the rest of the insult. The energy bolts punched holes straight through Swampfire's chest. The alien hero didn't even flinch.

When Manny stopped shooting, the holes in Swampfire's body healed themselves at once. Swampfire grinned. Now it was his turn.

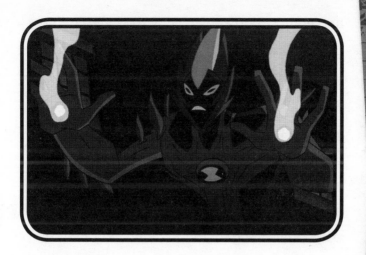

Throwing out his hands, Swampfire
unleashed a jet of blisteringly hot flames
straight at Manny. The four-armed alien
staggered backwards under the heat. He tried
to fight back, but Swampfire's blasts were too
powerful. With a groan, Manny buckled and
collapsed to the ground.

Swampfire turned to face the startled
Helen. 'Now,' he boomed, 'put down your
weapons and just listen for five minutes, OK?'

Helen hesitated, then slowly set her gun

and energy snare down on the pavement. 'All ears,' she said.

Half an hour later, Ben, Gwen and Kevin stood together. Helen and Manny stood beside them, still trying to understand everything they had just been told.

'So, we're all aliens?' asked Helen.

'Kinda,' shrugged Ben. 'One of your parents must've been human. The other – well, not so much.'

'Yeah?' demanded Manny, fiercely. 'Then how come you can switch back but we can't?'

Ben shrugged again. 'Luck of the draw.'

'But look at it this way,' smirked Kevin, staring up at Manny, 'your human version is probably even uglier.'

Manny clenched his fists. 'You wanna go another round?' he growled.

'Any time, pal.'

'Tell your boyfriend to back off,' Helen told Gwen.

'No, tell yours to . . .' Gwen began, before she realised what had been said. 'What? He's not my boyfriend!'

'Well you sure act like it,' said Helen.

'Don't tell me who my boyfriend isn't,' Gwen spluttered. She shook her head and quickly corrected herself. 'Is.'

'Think you're funny?' snarled Manny, prodding Kevin in the chest.

'Hey, you're the comedian. At least, you've got the face for it,' retorted Kevin.

Manny's breath hissed through his teeth. 'Boy, are you asking for it!'

'I'm begging for it,' said Kevin, raising his fists. 'Who's gonna give it to me?'

'I will, with three of my hands tied behind my back!'

'Hey, stop it. All of you,' cried Ben. He held up his hands. 'What am I? Your babysitter?'

Helen stopped arguing with Gwen and turned to look at Ben. 'You sound just like my brother,' she said. Sadness flashed across her face. 'Pierce was the one who always kept us grounded. The one who . . .'

She streaked away. In a heartbeat she was back, holding the hand-held video player. She held it up for the others to see. 'This is what he was talking about,' she said, switching the device on. They all stood in silence, watching Pierce talk about the alien who had been carrying the Plumber's badge.

'Don't you see, Manny?' Helen asked, when the video was done. 'We've been catching all those other aliens.'

'What other aliens?' frowned Ben.

Helen flicked a switch on the video gadget. Images of some of the aliens they had captured flashed up.

'Some of these might be other Plumber's kids,' Ben told them. 'Like us. Like you.'

'OK,' said Helen, decisively. 'In that case, we have to go into that . . . Uh, what was it you called it?'

'Null Void,' said Kevin.

'Null Void. Round up everyone we captured and free all the ones who shouldn't be in there.'

Manny snorted. 'Not a chance.'

Helen turned to face him. 'Well, Manny,

I'm doing it. Whether you come with me or not.'

'What? Why?'

'Because it's what Pierce would do.'

Manny glanced over at the Null Void Projector, then back to Helen. 'All right,' he nodded. 'For Pierce.'

Helen smiled and turned to face the others. 'Thanks,' she said. 'And sorry about . . .'

'Apology accepted,' said Kevin.

'Be careful,' Gwen told them.

'And good luck,' added Ben.

Manny and Helen approached the back

of the van. The swirling red of the portal flared brightly around them, and in a flash they vanished into the Null Void.

Kevin shook his head. 'That is so not gonna go well,' he said.

'I dunno,' said Ben, disagreeing. 'On paper we don't look like such a good team.'

'There is that,' Kevin admitted. He turned away. 'Now, if you'll excuse me, I'm gonna go swipe some of their equipment.'

'Kevin!' Gwen scolded.

'So not cool, man,' said Ben. He shook his head. Kevin might be one of the good guys now, but it seemed that some habits were harder than others to break!